# PHOTOGRAPHS

*Photographs by*
*H R H The Prince Andrew*

# PHOTOGRAPHS

## HRH THE PRINCE ANDREW

HAMISH HAMILTON · LONDON

First published in Great Britain 1985
by Hamish Hamilton Ltd
Garden House 57–59 Long Acre London WC2E 9JZ

Copyright © 1985 by H.R.H. The Prince Andrew

Book design by Craig Dodd

British Library Cataloguing in Publication Data

Andrew, Prince, son of Elizabeth II, Queen
   of Great Britain
   Prince Andrew photographs.
   1. Photography, Artistic
   I. Title
   779'.092'4        TR653

   ISBN 0-241-11644-9

Typeset by Rowland Phototypesetting Ltd, Bury St Edmunds, Suffolk
Printed in Great Britain by Balding & Mansell Ltd, Wisbech, Cambridgeshire
and bound by R. J. Acford Ltd, Chichester, West Sussex

# CONTENTS

# ACKNOWLEDGEMENT

The acknowledgement or, as the Oxford English Dictionary defines it, 'An author's statement of indebtedness to others', is possibly the hardest part of a book to write because there is always the inherent danger of forgetting someone or something.

As a first-time author, or perhaps more appropriately compiler/editor, there have been a great many people involved with the production of this book. They have striven to ensure that I produce something at least reasonably coherent. There are far too many to list by name here, however to everyone, and they know who they are, thank you for your time and patience.

There are a few who have been particularly helpful and I mention them here for special thanks: Firstly, Giles Gordon, who guided my pen in its wanderings around split infinitives and other traps waiting for me in the English Language, and secondly, Christopher Sinclair-Stevenson, the publisher, both of whom think I'm mad delivering a book and then, virtually immediately, sailing off to the South Atlantic and the Falkland Islands for five months, when most first-time authors are either biting their nails or ringing their publisher up every ten minutes.

Then there are the 'invisible people' in Buckingham Palace. In particular I would like to single out Adam Wise, my private secretary, who has played the very difficult role of anchor-man, co-ordinator and rearlink communicator between everyone involved in London and me 8,000 miles away in the Falklands.

There are then all the people who have been involved, either directly or indirectly, with me when I was taking the photographs during the past eighteen months: the camera, film and paper manufacturers for their support; the subjects of my photographs, particularly Finola Hughes, Clare Park and Kate Rabett for their various sufferings; Nick Read whose invaluable help in setting up some of the shoots was much appreciated; my policemen, who seem to get everywhere with me! Lastly in this list should be the Captain and the Wardroom in HMS *Brazen* who have all tolerated me and my photographs, and Steve Couling for correcting my spelling 'fairy well'.

Finally I am most indebted to Gene Nocon and his wife Liz who have had ideas and photographs bounced off them, thrown at them and pictures printed by me to get the mixture right in the final product. To Gene in particular my thanks for the complicated task of printing all the final photographs in this book, a very time-consuming task when I think of all the photographs I had to choose from. To him and everyone who has helped me, thank you.

# INTRODUCTION

This book is a compilation of photographs. They have been taken over a period of about eighteen months, since I bought myself a camera in the spring of 1983. It is also a small slice of autobiography recording memories and impressions through my eyes and the lens of a camera, although in this short introduction I have taken a few lines to try to explain how I became interested in photography and what led up to my trip to the shops, a rare visit for me, to buy a camera.

It is intended, above all, for the enthusiast and for the person who wants to 'have a go'. It is because I took my courage in both hands and 'had a go' that I have found such enjoyment in taking pictures. From a very early age, I have been exposed to cameras, their use, people taking pictures of my family, friends and myself. It does help, I admit, to have an exclusive location or two up your sleeve; there aren't that many people who would have the opportunity to photograph beautiful Fabergé or jade objets in the Royal Collection or the gardens of Buckingham Palace, but it is not really that important. You can make a picture even by having an empty room with only a light hanging from the ceiling. There are endless possibilities.

I hope that these pages will not be seen as 'how I did it' or 'how to take pictures of Royal palaces' but as a book by an enthusiastic amateur. For purely practical reasons I doubt whether I shall ever become another Noman Parkinson or Ansel Adams. Nothing would please me more should this book persuade more people to 'have a go'. I would like to try to bring photography out of the dark recesses occupied by professionals who take pretty pictures of girls for calendars. There is far more to photography than I will probably ever know.

Experimenting is fun: sometimes it works, sometimes it doesn't. For example, the section on macro-photography shows how I experimented with small, even tiny, items of jewellery. The jade lion on page 82 shows how I found that the position of the light in relation to the object helped or hindered the end result. Again, on pages 102 to 105, the photographs of model Clare Park illustrate how I wanted to create movement in a picture. Unfortunately it didn't work as well as I had hoped because of the long shutter speed. I made it increasingly difficult for myself, and Clare, by trying to get her to pirouette, hold her head still and look at the camera while at the same time creating the desired movement in the dress. The steps one has to take while discovering about light and shade, speeds and exposures, composition and experimenting are often infuriating. However when an experiment is successful the feeling of satisfaction is immense.

I joined the Royal Navy in 1979. In due course I went on to become a naval helicopter pilot, first flying Sea Kings and now a Lynx in HMS *Brazen*. After my training was completed I moved on to serve 'Frontline' in 820 Naval Air Squadron in October 1981. How soon it was that the designation 'Frontline' became all too true and real! In April 1982 we sailed south to the Falkland Islands in HMS *Invincible*. A considerable time was spent there, in and around the islands, during and after the conflict. It was during this time, particularly when the crisis was over, that I realised what a pity it was that I had no way of recording pictorially what was going on during those early days after the conflict, or the extraordinary events I had witnessed during the war. Peace, or the status quo, once again restored, the Argentinian soldiers looked dejected and faced a questionable future on being evacuated; the mess; the grime; the chaos; the number of people milling around in different uniforms, most of them with guns. It was a unique view. I wish I had had a camera with me to record everything that was going on.

At the beginning of 1983 we sailed in HMS *Invincible* across to the Caribbean to take part in both naval and military exercises. While there, I flew over jungle, over Jamaica, the Bahamas and over beautiful parts of the world which few people have an opportunity to see, particularly from the vantage point of a helicopter. In Belize I was partly responsible for flying around a photographer, while on one of the military exercises, who was doing a feature on 820 Naval Air Squadron and HMS *Invincible*. Once again I was made aware of a certain feeling of loss, because I did not have a camera myself. My interest in photography was aroused even further, in his technique, what he was doing and how he was doing it. I made a particular point to look at his pictures in a Sunday magazine some months later.

After Belize, and when I returned to the U.K., I realised it was high time that I bought myself a camera. The question was: what sort of camera should I get? I wanted something that could produce good pictures, which I could use efficiently and understand, or at least get a camera likely to last, stand up to a little bit of punishment and be capable of taking complicated pictures in both poor light and very bright conditions, such as we are used to in the Navy. After much deliberation and advice on the merits of a wide selection of camera makes, I eventually decided on a Nikon FE 2, which is a stainless steel-bodied camera and which has, over the last year and a half, survived some remarkable thumps and bumps in various parts of the world.

The next step in my development as a photographer, apart from my trial and error experimenting, came when Koo Stark, now Jefferies, came back to the U.K. with some pictures of herself, taken by Norman Parkinson, for printing. To get them printed she went to see photographic printer Gene Nocon. At this time Gene was organising an exhibition, to be held in October 1983, of photographs taken by people who were themselves the subjects of photographers. He invited her – as someone in public life and the subject of photographers – to take pictures of them taking pictures of her for his exhibition, called "Personal Points of View". Koo came to see me and suggested that I should take part as well. I replied that I was sure that I wouldn't be allowed to. Koo then went back to see Gene without my knowledge and asked him if a friend of hers could also take part. Although Koo was reluctant to name names and Gene was equally reluctant to agree to an unknown person taking part, it seems they came to an understanding because, as a consequence of all this secret negotiation, I was in Gene's office a week later with a load of film for him to develop, and after Gene had seen some of my work I was invited to take part in his exhibition "Personal Points of View".

# INTRODUCTION

To my surprise and delight no one at Buckingham Palace raised any objections, and that is essentially how I became involved in Gene's exhibition and how I became involved in photography as a whole.

The book is divided into sections showing how I have progressed from the complete beginner in "Windows, Roofs and Gardens" to the experiments of Macro-photography in "What's so bad about being an egg?", through some of the impressions I have gathered, at home, in "Summer Days and Sundays", abroad, in "Official Visits", and in my service life entitled "Things that go bump in the night" and "Off Duty". Near the end is what I think of as perhaps the more accomplished work, in the "Ilford Calendar Project", and finally to end the book some "Personal Pictures".

"Windows, Roofs and Gardens" which I have sub-divided into 'Buckingham Palace' and 'Windsor' shows that I started taking the majority of pictures through windows, from the roof and in the garden as I'd be less likely to be noticed with a camera. Then, in a sense having successfully practised and begun experimenting 'out of sight', I went to the United States of America and Northern Canada, where I became slightly more confident in my approach and felt that I could safely be seen with a camera.

There are times when I can relax and enjoy a quiet holiday away from inquisitive and prying eyes. One such time was in the summer of 1983, on the South Nahanni River in the North-West Territories. After my short stay in Newport, Rhode Island,, for the Americas Cup, I went north first to visit my old Canadian school, Lakefield College School, where I studied for two terms between January and June 1977, and then on to Yellowknife, to fly on to the South Nahanni River.

The opening picture of the section, 'Canada 1983', shows so much of what it was really like. Yes, there is beautiful scenery and yes, there are idyllic days, but for some reason while we were canoeing down the river, the weather wasn't on our side; in fact, it was positively against us. At times I wish I'd had a direct line to the Met. man in the sky. The introductory picture was taken on the expedition's first evening. We arrived at a point on a map, which turned out to be a beach of rocks called Rabbit Kettle, in a Royal Canadian Mounted Police Twin Otter airplane. There we found two canoes left for us by the rest of the party, a group of international students, all of whom were either at Lakefield or had just left at the end of the school year. We were to meet up with them at the place where this picture was taken. Soon after we arrived there, the weather began to deteriorate and, with only just enough time to pitch my tent, it began to rain. On this occasion I managed to get into my tent in the nick of time and sit out the very heavy rainstorm. As it passed overhead, I took some pictures from the door of my tent and, as you can see, the raindrops were not only frequent but very large, large enough to register on the film as streaks. It never ceases to amaze me to see the weather at work, and, as a pilot and sailor, I have great respect for it.

In Canada, the protection of visitors such as myself is carried out by the Royal Canadian Mounted Police. On the canoeing expedition I was accompanied by my RCMP bodyguard. One of my British

# INTRODUCTION

policemen came out to Canada to join me a couple of days before I returned to the U.K. We see a great deal of each other! He must spend about 40% of his 'on duty' life trying to keep tabs on me. Equally, I must spend 40% of my life trying to get away from him. But there are times when security is synonymous with blending into the environment. When we are by a lake and I am water-skiing, why shouldn't he try to catch a fish? It so happens that this is exactly what he did. After some time, trying to be inconspicuous, he caught one and as I happened to be passing at his moment of triumph I had to photograph the great catch! (I can assure you that he was after the suspicious one lurking about waiting to bite my unsuspecting toe. Oh, and he did put the little fish back!)

Some photographs are boring; some subjects are familiar to many people; others are of interest to only a small, select band of enthusiasts. The subject matter of, for instance, the Taj Mahal, the Pope, the Golden Gate in San Francisco is familiar to many. Other subjects are of interest to specialised groups of people – the landscape, portraits or still life. There is at least one picture in these pages which will be familiar to many people; one such is of a guardsman, although not perhaps quite like the one on page 21. A few of us, such as myself, live surrounded by guardsmen all the time. We see them at their best and also, it has to be said, we see their mistakes. To me – no doubt because I live with them around me – the usual picture of a sentry outside his box is uninteresting. One day in 1983 I received a telephone call to the effect that there was a possible suspect in the garden of Buckingham Palace; something that happens on the odd occasion! I made my way up to a discreet vantage point on the Palace roof, from where I could see quite a large area of the garden. A police helicopter flew overhead and over the garden. At the critical entry points into the Palace were guardsmen, still dressed in ceremonial uniform, but obviously not there only for picturesque purposes. I took some shots of one particular guardsman as the pictures would be quite different from what is normally seen. My first few shots show a guardsman at ease in a doorway. He was, naturally, quite unaware of being captured on film. My camera makes a noise with the motordrive and, as I took the pictures, the guardsman began to search for the 'noise'. He located it over his left shoulder and above him. There is nothing unusual in that, except that after I had developed and blown up the negative on the enlarger, I could see there was a broad grin upon his face which had been obscured by the chinstrap of his bearskin when I took the picture. At last I'd pictured a guardsman showing some form of human emotion, which many will know is something guardsmen shouldn't do – at least, not while on duty outside the front of palaces and castles.

Memories and impressions are a very important part of life and trying to remember things in years to come just from memory is quite difficult. "Summer Days and Sundays" is a selection of photographs taken not because I thought the view or subject was incredibly interesting or beautiful but rather because I wanted to keep alive the memory in a photograph: the peace and tranquillity of walking through a wood in summer carpeted with bluebells, watching sailing ships of past eras (even though the one

# INTRODUCTION

depicted is a Russian), of quietly sailing round the Western Isles off Scotland in the Royal Yacht passing Duart Castle on Mull and waving to the Laird; stopping off for the day at the Queen Mother's enchanting Castle of Mey before finally arriving at Balmoral for a few weeks' private holiday. After this annual recharging of our batteries it is back, once again, to the silly season.

Overseas tours are a major evolution in our family. There are months of painstaking planning and meetings before we leave to do the job. My first experience of a foreign tour was to Montreal in Canada for the 1976 Olympics. I was also fortunate enough to be included in the Royal tour of Africa in 1979. Since then I have been in the Royal Navy and the only times I have been abroad have been with the Navy, visiting foreign ports. On all these previous tours and port visits I had no camera.

However, last year I made my first major official overseas tour, to St Helena and Ascension Island. I was to represent Her Majesty at St Helena's 150th celebrations and, later, go on to Los Angeles. The journey from Britain to St Helena, a small island in the middle of the South Atlantic, is normally by sea from either Bristol or Capetown, in the Motor Vessel *St. Helena*, which takes about three weeks. I was fortunate in that I flew from RAF Brize Norton in the U.K. care of the airbridge to Ascension Island, taking a matter of hours, and from there by sea the 750 miles south to St Helena in HMS *Herald*. I wanted to take as many pictures as I could because few people get to see this beautiful island and its 5000 inhabitants. I allowed myself a morning to go around the island, visiting the house where Napoleon had lived, and to see the mists over the east side of the island. Sadly, I still didn't have enough time to do all the things that I wanted, but that is always inevitable on an official tour.

In Los Angeles the story was totally different. I hadn't realised it at the time, but I had a pretty gruelling schedule to maintain. I was kept so busy that I didn't get as many photographs as I would have liked. Besides, it would have been very odd to have seen a picture of myself in the newspapers with a huge camera strapped to my shoulder, or even using one while making an opening address would look fairly silly. I have included here some of the pictures from both tours to try to give a glimpse of the impressions I gathered.

The "Ilford Calendar Project" came about as a result of my involvement in "Personal Points of View". After the exhibition I was at a loose end with my photography. I had begun to learn to print my own pictures from Gene, and at the same time built a darkroom in an empty unused bathroom (of which there are a large number) at Buckingham Palace. The invitation from Ilford was made because they wanted an amateur to take the pictures for their 1985 Calendar. They also wanted it to help encourage other people and to promote black and white photography. I was delighted to be asked and even more delighted when my work was accepted. I will briefly describe here just two of the shots taken for the Calendar: "The 9th Wife", because it was probably the most difficult, and "Griffin House", because it was the first.

# INTRODUCTION

Griffin House is in the Strand, just a few yards from Trafalgar Square towards Charing Cross. The idea came to me because I had seen photographs of geometrical shapes. During December 1983 I would return to Buckingham Palace from Gene's workshop in Covent Garden by going down the Strand. On the way I had to pass Griffin House, which was always lit up at night to advertise its presence to potential customers as it was a new, and still empty, office block. I enquired who the owners were and asked their permission to view it and possibly to use it in a photograph. Quite by coincidence, the building facing it is Coutts Bank. I popped in one afternoon to ask the Managing Director if it would be possible to use his building to take the pictures from. (There were four of us seen escorted through the bank to the Managing Director's office. A few words of greeting were exchanged, then we turned out the lights to see better across the street. When we came out again, we got some very weird looks!)

With permission granted, we needed to find a suitable evening to take the shot. We chose the quietest day we could to avoid too many people being about: Boxing Day. We took a few photographs, some for fun as on page 110, to see exactly what was going on across the street. Direction was difficult, partly because of the distances involved but also because the windows in Griffin House don't open. Fortunately, we carry radios to communicate between policemen, so I sent one of my policemen with a radio across to be my communications link while I had one in the bank to give directions to the starring couple.

Incidentally, if you drive down the Strand today, you won't see Griffin House as I did because there is a new building between it and Charing Cross station which blocks the view I had from the Bank and from the street.

"The 9th Wife" – alias dancer and actress Finola Hughes – is the picture that has possibly created the greatest interest in all my photographs to date. After having taken the picture of the Dean of Windsor sitting in St George's Chapel in the Castle for the April slot in the calendar, he wrote to me saying that he would love to help me find another location. He added a P.S.: "How about the dungeons?" Here was a marvellous possibility to take a picture of a damsel in distress in a dungeon. I had difficulty in finding a volunteer gaoler: even my policemen didn't want to put on black leather trousers, oiled torso and hood. Cowards!

However that wasn't the greatest problem. When my assistant Nick Read went to see the dungeons he reported that they were, sadly, unsuitable as they had just been re-decorated and had a fresh coat of paint on the walls and new floor tiles. While in the Castle he asked if there was anything else that could be used instead. He was shown 'The Escape'. This is a staircase and tunnel from the Castle, under the town and out to the river. It was used in Mediaeval times. The entrance is a false floor in the Curfew Tower. It goes down some sixty feet, then turns sharp right, down a few more steps but then had been blocked up, as it is not supposed to be needed today, although I don't know . . .

There was another problem to overcome: total darkness. There was only a wall-mounted light and

# INTRODUCTION

that has long since given up the ghost. This is fine until you want to take a light reading for an exposure. You get nowhere, slowly. Having said that we'd try it, we arrived on another cold wet February afternoon and started to hump cameras and lights down into the dark tunnel. We had brought with us a five by four inch plate camera as well as the Hasselblad that I had recently been lent by my mother, as the five by four would give us so much more scope in the prevailing light conditions.

My idea was for a girl, queen or princess, to be trying to escape as it might have happened many centuries ago. With this in mind Zandra Rhodes very generously allowed us to borrow a fantastic black dress for Finola. She went up to the warmth of the Castle to change and wait until Gene, Nick and I had created some sort of organisation and light out of darkness. We spent some three hours down that tunnel, setting it all up. Then came the Ghost. Now I can't remember whose idea it was, but we started to see if we could make a superimposed image on the film to create a vision. This all came about because, in the course of setting up, Gene and I were discussing light in relation to distance and F.stop. (We worked out that if you took an exposure reading to arrive at a correct exposure then stop down one F.stop one has to expose the negative twice to compensate for the change; so to create an image or vision on the negative one exposes the person in only one of the exposures, eg. a reading giving a correct exposure of F16 would mean you would have to alter the F.stop to F22.) We, in fact, worked backwards to the final shot. We started with a 4-vision polaroid. It worked, but not very well, so we reduced from 3 through to 2-visions and then finally to 1. After our experimenting we brought Finola to the scene. I explained what I wanted from her. First, we were going to take a straight shot of her before we tried a Ghost. (This was in case it didn't work, so that we had an alternative picture.) She posed and joked splendidly in the dark, damp and cold. The policeman, as ever, couldn't stay away for long! Then we tried the Ghost. The first picture was with Finola in the frame. The second was at one stop difference and with her out of the frame. As it turned out, the picture did work, far better than we had ever envisaged.

I almost forgot; why is it called "The 9th Wife"? Well, this is one of those things that will have to remain a mystery; and there is quite a lot of mystery within the walls of the Castle.

It may be thought, by some, that I have all the time in the world to take photographs, to work on and improve my technique. Not so. I am a full-time naval officer and as such have to be dedicated to my job. Being a naval aviator means more than just possessing professional dedication. I fly a helicopter with only one set of flying controls. I am the only pilot. The man who sits next to me is an Observer. He handles the tactical use of the aircraft and the radar. Because of this my hands are taken up with the cyclic and collective flying controls, to fly the helicopter, which doesn't leave me with a free hand to take any pictures. However, there are opportunities to take photographs in my ship, a few of which are included in the section "Things that go bump in the night".

I will, probably, be a full-time naval officer for the foreseeable future, which means that most of my photographs have to be taken when I am off duty, away for weekends or on leave. The small section

# INTRODUCTION

"Off Duty" shows a little of the where and what of life that we see while we are away with the Service. These few are a selection from France, Italy and Sicily, taken during our last deployment, with NATO, in the Mediterranean.

Having said all that I have in this Introduction, there is just one more topic I must mention and that is the question of photographs of my family. Yes, there are some pictures of my family here because, as most beginners do, I have found people close to me to be excellent photographic subjects. This book is, after all, about my development as a photographer, not about my family, or anyone in particular. Furthermore, I must agree with those who regard the camera as intrusive, and have to admit that in taking photographs of my family and friends I have found, to my cost, that the mere presence of a camera can cause varying degrees of frustration and irritation!

Like any other photographer, I am conscious of trying not to get in the way of everyday private life in the attempt to obtain that 'great exclusive family shot', and of trying to resist saying too often, 'Sir, Sir, just one more!' My family has enough trouble from intrusive cameras without my wielding another. I am avoided whenever seen or heard with a camera. Unlike those who make it their living taking pictures of my family for the media, I have to live with my family.

I am, therefore, quite unrepentant that there are only a very few pictures of my family, and those that are there are included more because of the picture than simply because of the person being photographed. Every picture tells a story. I would ask you, if you would, to see this as a book by me, tyro-photographer, rather than by me, member of the Royal Family. I am the first to grant that some people would see this book as being published because of who I am. All the proceeds from the sale of this book will go to deserving causes and charities. Because of this or for whatever reason you have bought a copy, I have regarded it as a responsibility to see that the book is, in the widest possible sense, as entertaining and interesting as possible; and, I hope, will be an inspiration to amateur photographers.

FEBRUARY 1985

# WINDOWS, ROOFS AND GARDENS

SAFETY

3 → 3A

The photograph which introduces this section was the first picture I took with my new camera. The first half of this section contains photographs taken from various vantage points in and around Buckingham Palace, through windows, from the roof and in the garden. They were all taken from places where I knew I couldn't be seen. I wanted to learn how to use a camera, at least to start with, away from inquisitive eyes.

The subjects may appear highly conventional, but this is usually the case with beginners. I picked out views and events which I had regularly been watching over many years. My shots of the Changing of the Guard, of dogs and flamingoes in the garden, the Victoria Memorial (the Wedding Cake) at various times of the day or night, are not unlike all those snaps which are the beginnings for most photographers.

The second half of this section shows the same principles re-created at Windsor Castle, with pictures taken from inside through windows, and from the Round Tower looking into the quadrangle at the guardsman on duty; also shortly after when he was inspected by the duty officer.

The last photograph is of the Round Tower with a moon in the background. Because of the length of exposure, about one minute, I was able to get an almost daylight image. False moons in photographs look too sharp as the only way to print one is to use a coin. The moon in this picture, as you can see, is real as the edges are all blurred.

# CANADA

These pictures of Canada were taken the first time I ventured forth with a camera outside the closeted surroundings of home. To take any pictures at all I had to delve deep into my rucksack to get the cameras out; to keep them dry I had to protect them in waterproof bags, and, as the likelihood of my 'dumping' was ever present, in usually more than one bag. On one occasion I did go for an unscheduled swim, which took both of us in the canoe by surprise. Everything got wet as we were seen floating off down the river. Thankfully, the plastic waterproof bags did their job and saved my cameras from getting wet, so I was able to go on shooting.

The particular area we were in afforded endless stunning views and superb landscapes. Sadly, because I kept my cameras out of the way while we canoed during the day, I did not get as many photographs as I would have liked. It was truly Ansel Adams country, as I now know, but with my knowledge and inexperience, at that time, it was difficult to do justice to any of those magnificent views in one of my photographs.

# SUMMER DAYS
# AND SUNDAYS

This section includes pictures taken in the spring and summer of both 1983 and 1984. I was stuck for an introductory title for this group of photographs until, while looking through the photographs that I had chosen to go in this section, I realised that the majority were taken on a Sunday. At home, so much goes on during the other six days of the week that Sunday is usually the only day with enough time to spare to go out exploring with a camera.

Summers at home are spent first in the Royal Yacht for a week or ten days; the pictures of the Castle of Mey and Duart Castle were both taken on our way north. At Balmoral, the ptarmigan on page 76 is a good example of a Sunday picture. These wild and beautiful birds live high up on the slopes of the Scottish Highlands. It is a pleasant two-hour 'after Sunday lunch' walk up to the top of Loch na Gar from where you are quite likely to see a ptarmigan on the slopes of this gracious mountain.

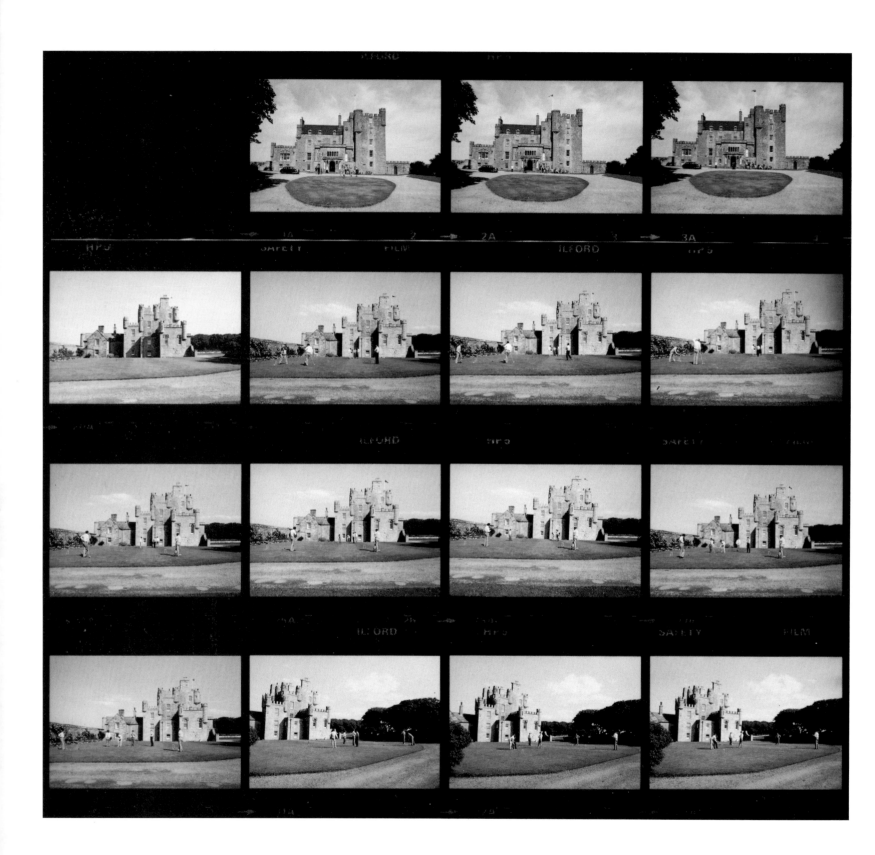

# 'WHAT'S SO BAD ABOUT BEING AN EGG?'

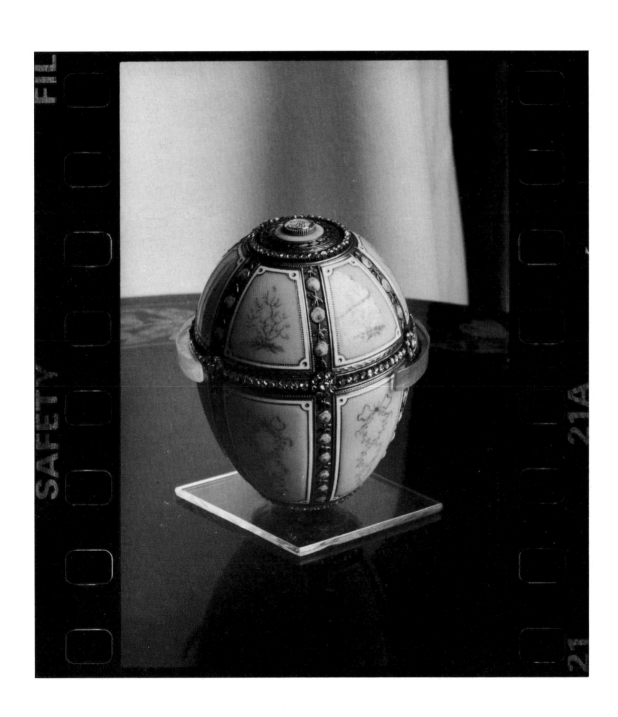

After my participation in Gene Nocon's exhibition, "Personal Points of View", my enthusiasm for photography didn't wane. I continued to experiment and take all sorts of pictures while also learning to print my own work.

For years I had been passing cabinets crammed with every kind of beautiful thing in the passages of Buckingham Palace. I asked to borrow the keys to some of these cabinets so that I could try my hand at taking photographs of close-up still life, using a macro-lens kindly lent to me by Gene. The objects were all either tiny bits of jewellery or miniature items of jade often by Fabergé. As you can see, they were very much an experiment as most weren't a brilliant success. I was only dabbling in this highly specialised field of macro-photography.

The end picture, of the angel in the egg, is interesting. I only discovered the angel by chance as I was about to take a photograph, because I dropped the said egg when I was getting it out of the cabinet. Fortunately I managed to catch it before it hit the floor and was damaged, but in the process it opened to reveal the exquisite tiny angel inside.

80

# OFFICIAL VISITS

As I said in the Introduction, a great deal of my family's year is taken up with official visits of one sort or another. They range from opening schools, making after-dinner speeches to fully-fledged overseas tours requiring meticulous planning and, to a certain extent, split-second timing.

This particular section covers the two official overseas visits I made in the spring of 1984. The first was to St Helena and Ascension Island, the second to the megalopolis of Los Angeles.

In Los Angeles I didn't have a great deal of time to myself, usually only at breakfast before I went out or later at tea time between the afternoon engagement and the evening one, so the only pictures I could take were from my hotel balcony.

St Helena, on the other hand, where I did have a little more time, was enchanting and strangely beautiful. Once seen, never forgotten. The windward side of the island is usually veiled in a thin mist from the prevailing wind, which picks up the moisture from the ocean on its long sea track from Africa. On the other side of the island it is dry and inhospitable, almost like a rocky desert. It is an island full of mystique and one with which I, for one, fell in love.

# THE
# ILFORD CALENDAR
# PROJECT

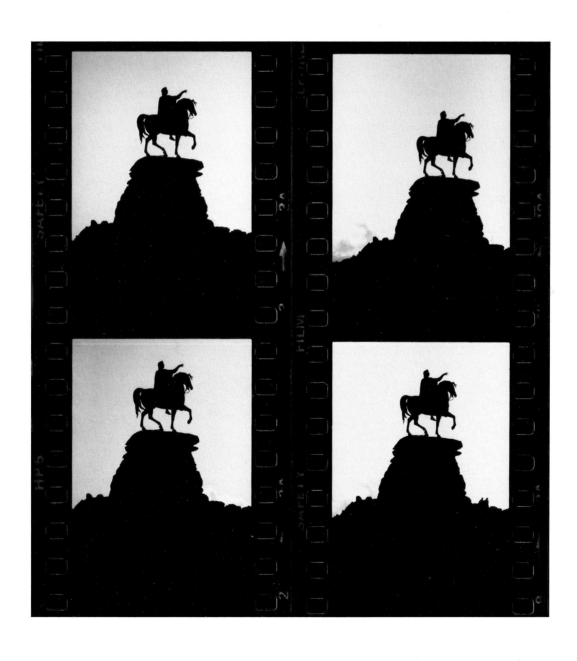

The "Ilford Calendar Project" was my next stage in photography. In this I was aided by a small team, all immensely talented and helpful to me. In this section are pictures considered for, but not used in, the calendar, along with the final outcome next to them. I have described the "9th Wife" and "Griffin House" in some detail in the Introduction.

The cover for the calendar was supposed to have been a picture of my camera in front of a sentry box, but on the day I chose to do it (a Sunday) it poured with rain so I had to scrub it. I had with me, by chance, a fish-eye lens to continue my experimenting. On this occasion, as it was raining, I went around the Castle taking the odd shot here and there. One of the shots ended up as the cover. It was also taken from where I could be easily overlooked by people visiting the Castle. To avoid them I got myself into position, stuck the camera through the balustrade at arm's length, and fired off a couple of frames. Much to my surprise I managed to get the picture and it ends this section.

The whole project took some weeks during January, February and March, as I was only able to take the photographs at weekends or when away from the Navy. This was a considerable handicap as not only was continuity lost, but it was also awkward trying to get people together on a Saturday or Sunday. It was difficult, but with some clever ideas from the Dean of Windsor and some sound advice from the team, it was eventually completed.

# `THINGS THAT GO BUMP IN THE NIGHT'

In this section I have included pictures taken during my time in the Navy since I first bought a camera, from the early days in HMS *Invincible* up to the last deployment to the Mediterranean, visiting France, Italy and Sicily in HMS *Brazen*. Opposite the picture of one of our Aircraft Carriers is a photograph of one of the Soviet Aircraft Carriers. We were on our way to take part in a major NATO exercise when we received orders to have a good look at this ship and its escort on their way to Murmansk. As you can see, their engines need more than a little maintenance and while on the subject you can see in the background a Sea King helicopter having a good close look.

You may be wondering why I called this section "Things that go bump in the night". Looking through the section I came to the picture of the Sea Harriers landing and it reminded me of flying operations in HMS *Invincible*, involving both Sea Harriers and Sea Kings. My cabin in the ship was directly below one of the helicopter landing spots. When I was tucked up in my bunk at night and the squadron was night flying, every time one landed on the spot above my head there was an enormous bump as the wheels hit the deck. Of course, some landings were softer than others!

# OFF DUTY

This section follows on from the last, as these pictures illustrate some of my impressions gathered while on my travels with the Royal Navy; for instance, in France, pictures of narrow streets from a small village in the south not far from Nice where I spent a happy hour or two wandering quietly around the village, up the tiny alleys and down the narrow streets.

The few pictures of the two young girls were photographed when I was in Palermo, Sicily. They were very animated and happy, and surprisingly quite at ease while I snapped away. It often pays to sit quietly, wait and observe one's surroundings. It certainly paid dividends in this case.

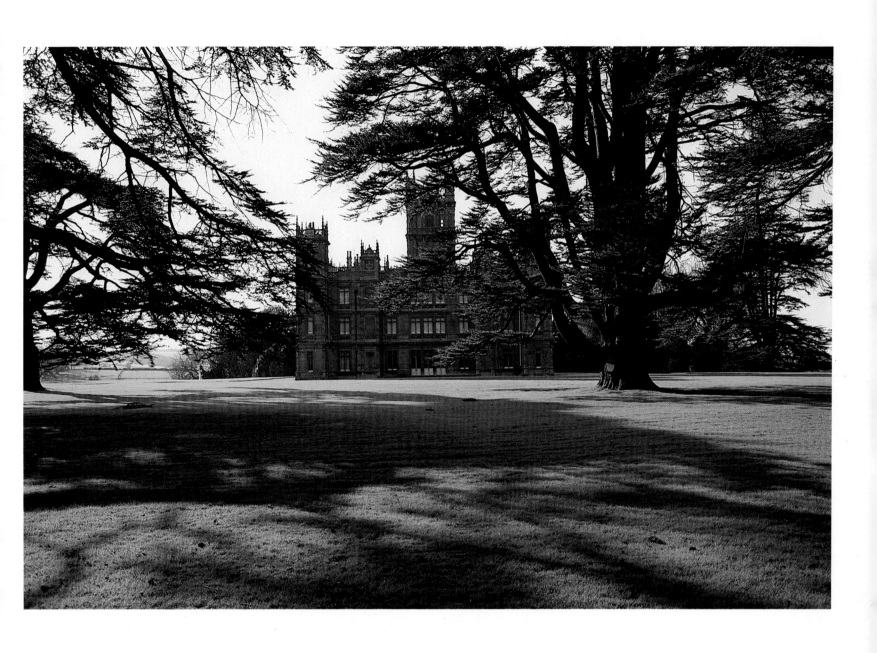

# PERSONAL PICTURES

This is the smallest section in the book and also the last.
I will simply introduce it as photographs of members of my family, taken when they were on guard
and aware of my presence with a camera.

Cameras: NIKON FE2; 8mm Fisheye, 55mm Macro, 85mm, 80–200mm Zoom HASSELBLAD 2000 FC;
50mm, 80mm, 150mm SINAR P; 150mm, 240mm
Lighting: BOWENS Quadmatic 2000
Film: ILFORD HP5
Processing and Printing: The Photographers' Workshop, London, England